Lucy Selby

SIMON AND SCHUSTER

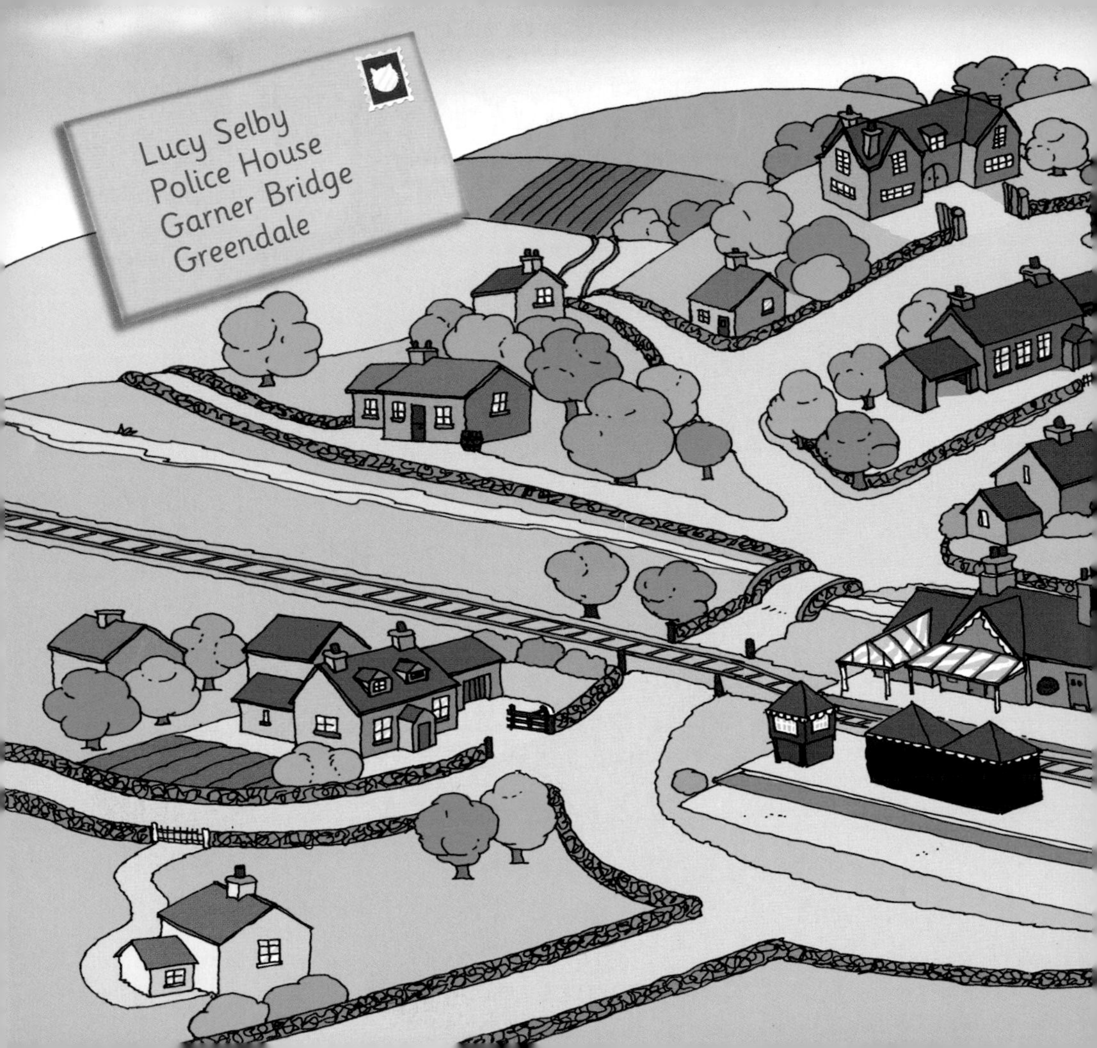
Lucy Selby
Police House
Garner Bridge
Greendale

Come and say hello to Lucy Selby!

PC Selby's dreamy daughter loves to spend hours reading storybooks and playing let's pretend. But when her dad runs out of mysteries to solve, Lucy makes it her job to put things right...

PC Selby's new panda car had finally arrived.

"It looks great, Dad!" grinned Lucy.

"Just think of all the cases I'll be able to crack with this vehicle," said PC Selby. "I'll be at the scene in seconds!"

Lucy nodded. "Especially now you've got a proper blue flashing light."

Her dad admired the car one more time. "Think I'll give it another quick polish before tea..."

POLICE

The next morning Postman Pat stopped by.

“Hello,” smiled Pat. “My, what an impressive vehicle.”

“Oh yes,” nodded PC Selby. “Look, it’s even got a special Greendale Police badge.”

Lucy gave Jess a cuddle, then climbed in the panda. “Dad’s giving me a lift to school.”

“Just a one-off, mind,” said PC Selby, “soon I’ll be too busy solving cases.”

POLICE

As soon as Mr Pringle rang the school bell, Lucy rushed home. She got back to find her dad shining up the panda's headlamps with a cloth.

"So, what adventures have you had today then?" she asked.

PC Selby rubbed his chin thoughtfully. "Um, well, er..., none."

"Oh," said Lucy. "Well, just imagine how busy you're going to be tomorrow!"

PC 1

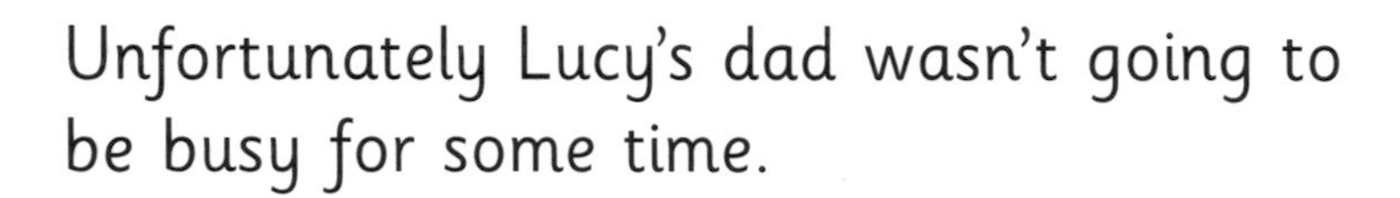

Unfortunately Lucy's dad wasn't going to be busy for some time.

"There hasn't been an untoward incident for days!" he moaned, staring at his police radio.

It had been a week, PC Selby was starting to get well and truly fed-up.

"There must be lots of cases to solve out there," comforted Lucy. "We just need to find them..."

The next day, Lucy told her best friend, Sarah, everything.

"Poor Dad'll go potty if he can't put that car to good use," Lucy explained.

"So that's why you've had your head in the clouds all afternoon," said Sarah.

Suddenly Lucy stopped in her tracks. "Hey! Look at Jess!"

"He's just sitting in the apple tree," shrugged Sarah.

"Sitting, or stuck?" said Lucy. "We need help!"

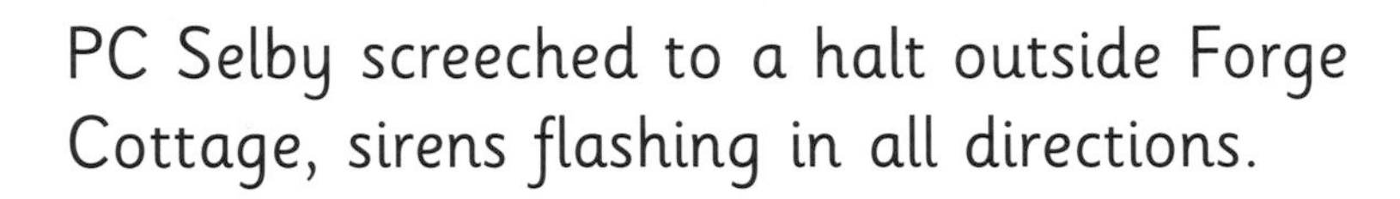

PC Selby screeched to a halt outside Forge Cottage, sirens flashing in all directions.

"Under six minutes, excellent!" he said, clearing his throat. "Now what appears to have occurred?"

"Jess is stuck up a tree, Dad!" cried Lucy.

Postman Pat wandered out to see what was up. "Not anymore folks."

Jess had hopped down and padded indoors for some peace and quiet.

PC 1

Everyday Lucy tried to find more helpful cases for her dad to clear up.

The Greendale kids made a call when Bill lost his anorak, but then he remembered that he'd left it at home.

Bonnie was reported for digging up Reverend Timms' flowers, until the vicar explained that the soil needed turning over anyway.

Things were going from bad to worse.

"I hear your dad's not getting out much in his new vehicle," said Pat, when he spotted Lucy in the village.

Lucy shook her head sadly. "He just wants to help people."

The pair stopped to let a row of ducks waddle across the lane.

"I think they might have given me a good idea," smiled Pat. "I just need to make a call to Jeff Pringle..."

"Morning, children," said PC Selby, the next day. "Mind the paintwork, won't you?"

Pat had found just the thing – PC Selby and his panda car were booked to teach road safety at Greendale Primary.

"Thanks, Pat," whispered Lucy. "You couldn't get a more helpful job for a policeman."

"Or a more helpful policeman's daughter," added PC Selby, grinning from ear to ear.

POLICE

SIMON AND SCHUSTER
First published in 2006 in Great Britain by Simon & Schuster UK Ltd.
Africa House, 64-78 Kingsway, London WC2B 6AH

Original writer John Cunliffe
From the original television design by Ivor Wood
Royal Mail and Post Office imagery is used by kind permission of Royal Mail Group plc

A CIP catalogue record for this book is available from the British Library upon request

ISBN 1416916482
EAN 9781416916482
Printed in China
1 3 5 7 9 10 8 6 4 2